LEADERS LIKE

# HENRY LOUIS GATES Jr.

BY J. P. MILLER

ILLUSTRATED BY
MARKIA JENAI

 Rourke
Educational Media

A Division of
Carson Dellosa Education

# BEFORE AND DURING READING ACTIVITIES

## Before Reading: *Building Background Knowledge and Vocabulary*

Building background knowledge can help children process new information and build upon what they already know. Before reading a book, it is important to tap into what children already know about the topic. This will help them develop their vocabulary and increase their reading comprehension.

### Questions and Activities to Build Background Knowledge:

1. Look at the front cover of the book and read the title. What do you think this book will be about?
2. What do you already know about this topic?
3. Take a book walk and skim the pages. Look at the table of contents, photographs, captions, and bold words. Did these text features give you any information or predictions about what you will read in this book?

### Vocabulary: *Vocabulary Is Key to Reading Comprehension*

Use the following directions to prompt a conversation about each word.

- Read the vocabulary words.
- What comes to mind when you see each word?
- What do you think each word means?

> ### Vocabulary Words:
> - *ancestors*
> - *DNA*
> - *doctorate*
> - *family tree*
> - *genealogy*
> - *obituary*
> - *paternal*
> - *slavery*

## During Reading: *Reading for Meaning and Understanding*

To achieve deep comprehension of a book, children are encouraged to use close reading strategies. During reading, it is important to have children stop and make connections. These connections result in deeper analysis and understanding of a book.

###  Close Reading a Text

During reading, have children stop and talk about the following:

- Any confusing parts
- Any unknown words
- Text to text, text to self, text to world connections
- The main idea in each chapter or heading

Encourage children to use context clues to determine the meaning of any unknown words. These strategies will help children learn to analyze the text more thoroughly as they read.

When you are finished reading this book, turn to the next-to-last page for **Text-Dependent Questions** and an **Extension Activity**.

# TABLE OF CONTENTS

# TRACING FAMILY ROOTS

Who are you? Your history is more than your name. It is more than the names of your family members who are alive today. It goes further back in time. Who were your **ancestors**? Dr. Henry Louis Gates Jr. wanted to help people learn about their ancestors. He wanted to help people understand their family history.

In a television studio, Henry Jr. waited behind the scenes. He was about to begin filming his show, *African American Lives*. He was going to help his first guest discover who their ancestors were. He was a leader in **genealogy**.

He had a lot of information to share. He was about to help many more people than just the ones on his show.

# A TRIP TO THE ATTIC

The house was filled with family. Everyone was there after young Henry Jr.'s grandfather died. Henry Jr. followed his father up the stairs. It was his first time in his grandparents' attic.

His father, Henry Sr., opened an old trunk. Inside were newspaper clippings and other Gates family treasures. He searched the stacks of papers until he found the **obituary** of his great-great-grandmother, Jane Gates.

Henry Jr. read the article. It said that his great-great-grandmother was a good parent and that people liked her. It talked about how both black and white people respected her. It listed all of Jane Gates's children. But it did not say who the father of her children was.

The trip to the attic changed Henry Jr. He became curious. He had questions about his **paternal** family. Henry Jr. set out to solve the mystery: Who was his great-great-grandfather?

Henry Jr. made a special trip to the store to buy a spiral notebook. He was going to interview his family. He planned to write what they said in his notebook. His family was happy that he was interested in his **family tree**. They sat with him and **shared funny stories,**

**...family celebrations,**

**...and pictures.**

Henry Jr. wrote it all down. He learned a lot about his family history. Still, there was something missing.

**Roots and Trees**
Family trees can be very important. They can help people understand their roots—how they are related to others. Some people even find out they are related to someone famous!

Henry Jr. grew up. He left home for college. Researching family trees still excited him. He knew what he wanted to study—history! He did very well in college. He was asked to teach classes while he was still a student! He earned a **doctorate** in history. Soon, he was famous for his research.

Henry Jr. watched a television show where a man traced his family tree all the way back to Africa. How did he do it, Henry Jr. wondered? He had tried, but he had no luck finding his great-great-grandfather. His family's history was missing information about when relatives were taken due to **slavery**. Other African American people wanted to discover their family trees too. He could become a leader and help people find their family history.

# SOLVING MYSTERIES

Tracing family trees back to Africa was all Henry Jr. thought about. He spent day and night thinking of ways to do it. Suddenly, he had an idea. He could use **DNA**. It could be used to trace the family history of famous African American people all the way back to Africa. He spoke to people at PBS Television about his idea for a show. He was already a leader in history. Now he wanted to be a new kind of leader too.

PBS turned his idea into a television series called *African American Lives*. On each episode, Henry Jr. would get information from each famous guest. He found out as much as he could about their family tree using official documents.

He used information from the guest's DNA to learn more after that. He could finally tell people who their ancestors were. No other show was like this. He would lead the way once more.

Henry Jr. had many famous people on his show. He had eight guests the first time he made *African American Lives*. When he was done, he knew he could help many more people learn about their family history.

**Famous Faces**
One of the people that Henry Jr. interviewed was Oprah Winfrey, a famous talk show host. Other guests included comedians and scientists.

Henry Jr. never found out who his great-great-grandfather was. But his search led him to change lives. He has won many awards for genealogy research. He has written books and articles. Many people started to research their family history because of him. Henry Jr. gave hope to black people in Africa and America. He led them to learn their own family's stories.

"We all have ancestors waiting to tell our family's story. It is my job to find those ancestors on your family tree... open the door, and let them talk.
—Henry Louis Gates Jr.

# TIME LINE

1950 Henry Louis Gates Jr. is born September 16th in Keyser, West Virginia.

1973 Henry Jr. graduates summa cum laude and Phi Beta Kappa from Yale University with a BA in History.

1973 Henry Jr. becomes the first African American to receive the Andrew W. Mellon Foundation Fellowship. He is allowed to study at the University of Cambridge in the United Kingdom. He receives a PhD in English Language and Literature.

1975–1976 Henry Jr. begins his career at Yale University in the Afro-American Studies Department. He is offered the job of Assistant Professor once he finishes his doctoral degree.

1976 Henry Jr. is named a lecturer in English and African American Studies and the Director of Undergraduate Studies.

1988 Henry Jr. releases the award-winning textbook *Signifying Monkey: A Theory of Afro-American Literary Criticism.*

1991 to Present Henry Jr. is named a Professor and Director of the W.E.B. DuBois Institute for African and African American Research at Harvard University.

2006 Henry Jr. writes and produces the PBS documentary *African American Lives*. It is the first documentary series to use genealogy and genetic science to better understand African American history.

2008 Henry Jr. co-founds The Root, a website dedicated to African American perspectives.

2010 Henry Jr. hosts the PBS series *Faces of America*, learning the genealogy of 12 North Americans of different backgrounds.

2012–2016 Henry Jr. hosts three seasons of the PBS series *Finding Your Roots with Henry Louis Gates, Jr.*

# GLOSSARY

**ancestors** (AN-ses-turs): members of your family who lived long ago

**DNA**: material inside your cells that carries information about your body, some of which comes from your parents; can be collected for testing from saliva and blood

**doctorate** (dahk-tur-IT): a degree given to someone who has taken many years of specialized classes

**family tree:** (FAM-uh-lee tree): a diagram that shows how all the members of a family are related, going back many generations

**genealogy** (jee-nee-AL-uh-jee): the study of family history over many generations

**obituary** (oh-BIT-yoo-air-ee): an article written about a person after they die

**paternal** (puh-TUR-nuhl): related through a father

**slavery** (SLAY-vur-ee): a system in which some people claim to own others and force them to work

# INDEX

# TEXT-DEPENDENT QUESTIONS

1. What did Henry Louis Gates Jr.'s father show him in the attic?

2. What family member was Henry Jr. in search of?

3. What documents did Henry Jr. use in his research?

4. Why might it have been important for Henry Jr. to make a television show about his research?

5. How do you think *African American Lives* changed what people thought of genealogy?

# EXTENSION ACTIVITY

Pick a person in your family to interview about their family tree. Find out where their relatives came from. Locate each of the places on a map. Label the map with the name of the place and the family member that lived there.

# ABOUT THE AUTHOR

**J. P. Miller** is a debut author in children's picture books. She is eager to write stories about little- and well-known African American leaders. She hopes that her stories will augment the classroom experience, educate, and inspire readers. J. P. lives in Metro Atlanta, Georgia, and enjoys playing pickleball and swimming in her spare time.

# ABOUT THE ILLUSTRATOR

**Markia Jenai** was raised in Detroit during rough times, but she found adventure through art and storytelling. She grew up listening to old stories of her family members, which gave her an interest in history. Drawing was her way of exploring the world through imagination.

www.rourkeeducationalmedia.com

Quote sources: "Henry Louis Gates, Jr. Reveals Seth Is Kevin Bacon's Cousin." Late Night with Seth Meyers, February 12, 2019.


Edited by: Tracie Santos
Illustrations by: Markia Jenai
Cover and interior layout by: Rhea Magaro-Wallace

**Library of Congress PCN Data**

Henry Louis Gates / J. P. Miller
(Leaders Like Us)
ISBN 978-1-73163-800-7 (hard cover)
ISBN 978-1-73163-877-9 (soft cover)
ISBN 978-1-73163-954-7(e-Book)
ISBN 978-1-73164-031-4 (ePub)
Library of Congress Control Number: 2020930201

Rourke Educational Media
Printed in the United States of America
02-17822119337